The
Grizzly Sisters

Cathy Bellows

Macmillan Publishing Company   New York

Collier Macmillan Canada   Toronto

Maxwell Macmillan International Publishing Group
New York   Oxford   Singapore   Sydney

To Grandma Rose

Macmillan Publishing Company
866 Third Avenue
New York, NY 10022
Collier Macmillan Canada, Inc.
1200 Eglinton Avenue East
Suite 200
Don Mills, Ontario M3C 3N1
First edition
Printed in Hong Kong

10 9 8 7 6 5 4 3 2 1

The text of this book is set in 16 point Horley Old Style.
The illustrations are rendered in watercolor.

Library of Congress Cataloging-in-Publication Data
Bellows, Cathy.
The Grizzly sisters / Cathy Bellows. — 1st ed.
p.   cm.
Summary: The Grizzly sisters continually disobey their mother's
warning to stay away from other animals, and when they go near the
tourists they regret it.
ISBN 0-02-709032-9
[1. Grizzly bear—Fiction.   2. Bears—Fiction.]   I. Title.
PZ7.B415Gr   1991
[E]—dc20   90-38787

Sniff. *Sniff.*

Mama was a very cautious bear. Every morning, before she let her cubs out, she'd poke her head out the door of the den and sniff.

She sniffed north and south. She sniffed east and west. She sniffed high and low, and when she was finished she knew exactly who was in the forest and exactly where they were.

One morning, after she'd had a good sniff, Mama turned to her cubs and said, "My dears, you may play in the woods, you may play by the caves, but please, my darling grizzlies, don't go near the river. The beavers are out today and there are quite a few of them." Then she took another sniff. "Yes, seven to be exact, not including the baby."

So the Grizzly sisters skipped outside to play in the woods. They nibbled on twigs and tumbled in the leaves, and they played their favorite grizzly game. Roaring and stomping, they ran about through the forest and scared all the squirrels into the trees. Oh, it was great fun being a grizzly, especially when you could run about.

But bears are easily bored, and it wasn't long before they began to think about those beavers. "Why should we be afraid of beavers? They're not much bigger than squirrels." Then, very carefully, they tiptoed to the river, just to get a little peek.

Sure enough, there were seven little beavers (not including the baby). Well, the Grizzly sisters looked at each other and grinned a very grizzly grin.

"Shall we?"

"Dare we?"

"We really shouldn't."

But they did, anyway. They ran through the trees, roaring and growling and showing their claws.

When the beavers saw them, they slapped their tails in the water and sounded the alarm. "Grizzlies!" they cried. "Everybody, duck!" All eight beavers (including the baby) dived into the water and hid.

The Grizzly sisters were thrilled. It was most rewarding. Who would have thought they were so ferocious, so powerful? They stood on the riverbank and jumped for joy.

"We're big!"

"We're bad!"

"We're the Grizzly sisters!"

Then they ran home quickly, for they didn't dare be late for supper. Mama didn't like it.

"Honeycakes?" said Mama as her grizzlies came through the door.

"Honeycakes!" screeched the bears. Why, that was their favorite dinner. And they gobbled those cakes down.

Early the next morning, Mama poked her head
out the door, and once again she began to sniff.

She sniffed north and south, east and west, high
and low, and when she was finished she said, "My
dears, you may play in the woods, and you may play
by the river, but please, my darling grizzlies, don't
go near the caves. There are wolves near the caves."
She took another sniff. "Yes, either one big wolf or
two little ones."

So the Grizzly sisters went into the woods,
laughing and tumbling and running about. And it
wasn't long before, lo and behold, they found
themselves near the caves.

"Well, why shouldn't we have a peek at those wolves?" they asked. "After all, we're grizzlies, and when we run about we scare everybody to death."

Very carefully, they tiptoed toward the caves. And there, standing near the big rocks, they caught sight of two ferocious looking pups. The wolves had sharp teeth and long claws, but the Grizzly sisters weren't the least bit afraid. They hid in the bushes, and when the Wolf brothers came strolling by, the sisters jumped up and began to stomp and growl.

"We're big!"

"We're bad!"

"We're the Grizzly sisters!" Then they roared and clawed and shook their shaggy fur.

Well, the Wolf brothers weren't afraid of long claws, and they weren't afraid of sharp teeth, but all that shaking of shaggy fur scared them silly. "Mama!" they howled. "Papa!" And into the woods they disappeared.

The Grizzly sisters were simply delighted. "Wow! We really are quite ferocious." They looked at each other, and they couldn't help grinning.

"We're so great!"

"We're so powerful!"

"We're so grizzly!" And they made such ferocious faces that they practically scared themselves to death.

Of course now they had to run fast to make it
home for dinner. It would never do to be late.
Mama might get cross.

"Honeycakes, anyone?" said Mama as the
grizzlies sat down to eat.

"Yes!" said the sisters, and they gobbled them
down.

The next morning, as always, Mama went to the door to sniff. Only this time she took one little sniff and let out a growl. Quickly she pulled her head back inside, shutting the door tight.

"I'm very sorry, my dears, but there are tourists by the concrete road, and you mustn't go out at all today."

"But, Mama," cried the grizzlies, "couldn't we play by the den?"

"No!" said Mama. "It's much too dangerous. People and bears just don't mix. Unfortunately, however, *I* must go out, for we're very low on honey. Now, give your mama a kiss, and promise me you won't open the door for anything."

"We promise," said the grizzlies. And they kissed their mama good-bye.

Well, the Grizzly sisters played inside for a while, but, being bears, they became bored. Why shouldn't they go outside, they wondered. "We certainly have nothing to be afraid of. After all, we're grizzly bears." Then they growled their grizzliest growl.

True, they had promised their mama not to open the door, but they hadn't said anything about the windows. So, after much squeezing and pushing, the Grizzly sisters were on the loose.

And where did those bears go? To the concrete road, where else? They just had to get a little peek at the awful tourists.

Sure enough, the road was lined with cars, and there were people everywhere. Each one carried a camera, and they all were taking pictures. They took pictures of squirrels and trees and mountains. But mostly they took pictures of one another. Oh, it was the silliest thing the grizzlies had ever seen.

"Let's give them something good to snap at," they whispered. Then the Grizzly sisters grinned that terrible grizzly grin. They sharpened their long claws, and they shined up their sharp teeth. And after thoroughly shaking out their shaggy fur, those grizzly bears were ready.

Out of the forest they leaped, howling and growling and running about.

"We're big!"

"We're bad!"

"We're the Grizzly sisters!"

The tourists froze. Only the hair on their heads moved, as it stood up on end. There was complete silence.

Then a strange thing happened. The people began to smile. "Look!" they cried. "Grizzlies! At last!" And grabbing their cameras, they started clicking and snapping and taking pictures like crazy.

"Goodness gracious!" growled the grizzlies. "These people have no sense at all." The sisters tried roaring and stomping and clawing and shaking their shaggy fur, but it was no use. The grizzlier the grizzlies became, the more the people liked it, and the more people came.

Soon the concrete road was full of cars, horns honking and brakes screeching, and the people began to push and shove and yell and holler. They became such a wild horde that, finally, the Grizzly sisters could stand it no more. "Yipes!" they cried. "Let's get out of here!"

They ran through the forest as fast as they could. But wherever they went, the people followed.

"Grizzlies!" the tourists yelled. "Give us a growl!"

"Stand on your hind legs!"

"Show us your sharp teeth!"

The poor Grizzly sisters were terrified. They climbed up a tree and hid in the branches. But still those cameras clicked.

"Help!" they cried. "We're not so big! We're not so bad! We're only little bears! Go away!"

And as they sat in the tree crying, all of a sudden from the distance came the sound of rolling thunder. The ground began to tremble. The trees began to shake.

The tourists looked up at the sky, for they thought a storm was coming. But it was no storm.

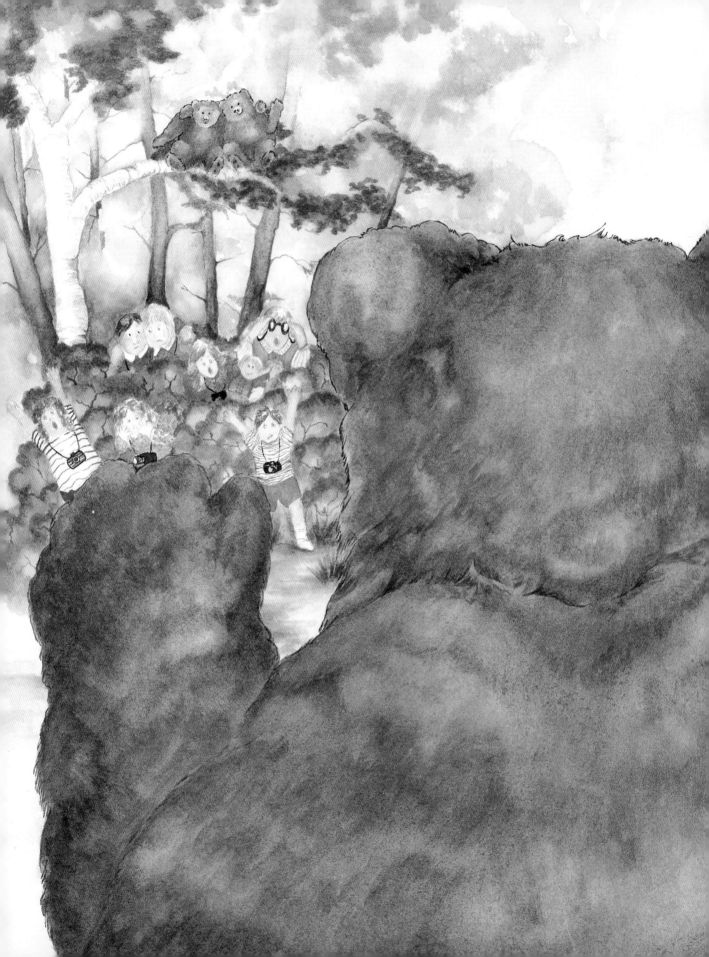

It was the all-sniffing, the all-knowing, the all-powerful grizzly. It was Mama Bear, and—wow!—was she ever mad.

Through the forest she stomped. "Who's chasing my babies?" she roared.

The people never answered. In a flash, the entire horde were back in their cars. With horns honking and tires screeching, down the concrete road they disappeared.

Mama, however, wasn't finished. After she'd helped her cubs out of the tree, she roared once more. "No honeycakes for you tonight!"

But the Grizzly sisters didn't care. They were so tired and so happy to be in Mama's arms that they fell fast asleep.

Early the next morning, they were up at the crack of dawn, up before Mama. They poked their heads out the door and began to sniff. They sniffed to the north. They sniffed to the south. They sniffed east and west, high and low, and when they were finished, they knew exactly who was in the forest and exactly where they were.

And when Mama awoke, she heard the sounds of cautious bears. "From now on, my darling grizzlies," she said, "you may go wherever you choose."

So out the door went the Grizzly sisters. *Sniff.*
Sniff. Sniff. Sniff.